Deathbird of Paradise

ERNEST HERNDON

ZondervanPublishingHouse
Grand Rapids, Michigan

A Division of HarperCollins*Publishers*

7216

For Alaina, Grant, Laura,
Susanna, and Julia Seabourne

Deathbird of Paradise
Copyright © 1997 by Ernest Herndon

Requests for information should be addressed to:

📖 ZondervanPublishingHouse
Grand Rapids, Michigan 49530

Library of Congress Cataloging-in-Publication Data

Herndon, Ernest.
    Deathbird of paradise / Ernest Herndon.
        p. cm. — (Eric Sterling, secret agent)
    Summary: On assignment for Wildlife Special Investigations, Eric
Sterling and his partners Erik and Sharon go to New Guinea to stop a
native poacher who is threatening endangered species.
    ISBN: 0-310-20732-0 (pbk. 0
    [1. Papua New Guinea—Fiction. 2. Adventure and adventureers—
Fiction. 3. Wildlife conservation—Fiction.] I. Title. II. Series:
Herndon, Ernest. Eric Sterling, secret agent.
PZ7.H43185De   1997
[Fic]—dc 21   96–50250
                                                          CIP
                                                          AC

Illustrations by Gloria Oostema

Printed in the United States of America

---

97 98 99 00 01 02 03 04 /❖ DH/ 10 9 8 7 6 5 4 3 2

1

Sunday morning I woke up grumpy. It was raining outside, and I didn't feel like going to church.

"You know we're having that guest speaker today," my mother said, trying to cheer me up, "the missionary from New Guinea."

Great. Maybe he'd show slides so I could sleep while the lights were out.

He didn't. Our church helped support the missionary, Roy Williams, and he was giving us some kind of annual report. It wasn't like a slide show with big adventure stories or anything.

Brother Roy looked about forty. He was thin and bald but very tan, I guess from living in the tropics. He introduced the audience to his wife, Pam, who

3

was also slender and tan with long brown hair. He said he and his wife lived in a town called Wewak on the New Guinea coast.

Then he started talking about budgets and membership and stuff, and I tuned out. But words drifted through my ears now and then. "New Guinea . . . second largest island in the world . . . rugged mountains . . . jungle . . . Stone-Age people . . . once cannibals . . . more modern now . . . still primitive . . ."

In the foyer after church, Brother Roy sold copies of a book he had written. The money went to his mission work.

Up close he didn't look as boring. His eyes twinkled with adventure. He gave me a firm handshake as I filed past.

"Eric's done a lot of traveling," Dad bragged.

"Is that right?" Brother Roy said. "Ever been to New Guinea?"

"No sir. But I have been to the South Pacific."

"Really? Where?"

"I went to the island of Baru one time, near Guam." I didn't tell him I had gone as a secret agent for Wildlife Special Investigations, a branch of the CIA.

"Great! You'll have to come to New Guinea and see us sometime."

Then I shook his wife's hand. She was pretty, with warm brown eyes and a smile that made me feel like she'd known me for a long time.

4

"Yes, come by and see us sometime, Eric," she said, squeezing my hand.

I smiled. "I will if I ever get over that way."

Of course, the chances of that were slim to none. But it was fun meeting them and finding out they were pretty cool.

When we got to the car, Mom handed me a copy of Roy's book. "I got this for you," she said. "You might want to do a book report on it someday."

"Thanks."

The title was *The Making of a Missionary*. The cover photo showed a man shooting a bow and arrow. He wore a loincloth and had pig tusks in his nose.

It was still raining, so after lunch I took the book to my room. Even though it wasn't a kid's book, I figured I'd check it out. In the middle were photos of natives, thatched huts, missionaries, mountains, and airplanes. I turned to the first page and started reading.

Next thing I knew, Mom was knocking on the door. "Eric, come eat, then we need to get ready for church."

Eat? Church? I glanced at the clock and realized the whole afternoon had passed! I was so wrapped up in the book I hadn't noticed.

I didn't want to stop reading. I knew missionaries had interesting stories to tell sometimes, but this one was wild!

Reluctantly I ate supper and attended evening

service. The Williamses had gone on to another church, which was too bad because I would have asked them questions about their adventures. As soon as I got home I took a quick bath and jumped into bed with the book. Since it was summer and school was out, my folks didn't mind me staying up late reading. It was after midnight when I finished. I put the book down, closed my eyes, and dreamed I was being chased by cannibals.

When I woke up I knew what I wanted to do: Write a book report.

I know, it's crazy to write a book report in the summer. But with it fresh on my mind, it would be easy to do. Then I could stick it in my drawer and have it aced for next school year. Smart, huh?

After breakfast I went to work. Here's what I wrote:

The Making of a Missionary by Roy Williams
A Book Report by Eric Sterling

Roy Williams is a missionary for my church. Many years ago he was a journalist visiting New Guinea. New Guinea is a big island divided into two countries. The one he went to is called Papua New Guinea.

Roy went on a bush patrol (jungle trip) with a missionary named Powers Stivell. Pam Carpenter also went. She was from Canada and was thinking about being a missionary. Roy believed in God but wasn't really a Christian.

They went up a river in a canoe. It was hot, and there were bugs. They tried to hire carriers to take them over the mountains, but no one wanted to. Everyone was afraid of the tribe that lived in the mountains because they used to be cannibals. Powers, Roy, and Pam finally dumped some of their food and stuff and went anyway. They had a guide named Yalu. He was part of the tribe of former cannibals. They were called Kukukukus.

The walk was very hard. It took many days. The mountains were so steep they had to hold on to branches to pull themselves up. There were leeches, which suck your blood. And then they came to a place with dead bodies hanging from trees. Really. They stunk. Powers said the way Kukukukus bury people is to stick them up in trees and let them rot. Pam got sick. I think I would have too.

At the village, people were friendly at first. But then the guide, Yalu, turned against them and told everyone else not to help them. They were stranded. They tried to signal an airplane but there weren't any. Powers got into an argument with Yalu and then something awful happened. I don't want to give anything away, but I guess I have to say that Powers got killed.

Roy and Pam ran into the jungle to get away. They didn't have anything. Well, Roy had a compass with a whistle and matches inside. Also a pocket knife. They fell down the side of a mountain. Lucky for them, because Yalu couldn't find them. At first, anyway.

They were scared. Roy got malaria. They were very hungry too. They ate leaves and stuff. They used Roy's compass to hike through the jungle, but the mountains were steep and also there was a river. It flooded and almost drowned them. But they fell in love, which is weird, to be running from a cannibal and find romance too. Roy started believing in Jesus, and Pam baptized him in a pool.

Roy made a spear and went hunting and a giant bird attacked him. The bird is called a cassowary. It doesn't fly. It grows six feet tall and can kill a person with its claws. It rips your guts out. Roy stabbed the bird with his spear and was happy because now they had meat. But then Yalu jumped out.

I don't want to give anything away, but I guess I have to say that Yalu got killed. Roy knew some kenpo, which is like karate. Anyway, he was sorry, but there was no choice.

He and Pam made it to town and everybody was sad because Powers was dead. But there was a happy ending because Roy and Pam got married and decided to be missionaries.

And it's true because I met them at church,

and they seemed like they're living happily ever after. Only it's hard to imagine them running through the jungle and fighting cannibals and falling in love and stuff because they are like forty years old or something. But all those adventures happened many years ago when they were young. Now they are missionaries and I guess they have adventures but not that kind. I guess.

The End.

Mom said it was the best book report I'd ever written and wanted to know why I didn't write them like that when school was in session. I told her that in school we never get to read books about cannibals and giant birds.

So I stuck the report in my drawer and forgot about it—until something really strange happened a couple weeks later.

2

Miss Spice sent her driver to pick up Ax and Sharon and me for a new secret agent assignment. I hadn't seen Ax and Sharon much lately. He was busy with karate, as usual, and his sister Sharon was working a lot with her dad, a veterinarian at the city zoo. I'd been hanging out at the mall or playing with my computer.

Usually when we walked into Miss Spice's office at Wildlife Special Investigations headquarters, she greeted us with a big smile and a platter of snacks. Today there was no smile, and I didn't see any snacks, either.

"Kids," our pretty, red-haired boss began, frowning, "I am not happy about this assignment."

"Uh-oh," I muttered as we sat down. "If Miss Spice isn't happy, ain't noooobody happy."

"I've racked my brain for the best way to handle this problem," Miss Spice continued. "I really wish I didn't have to send you three at all. Unfortunately, there just doesn't seem to be any other way."

"What is it?" Ax asked, sounding excited. He would be. He's a black belt whose biggest thrill is karate tournaments. The scarier it is, the more he likes it.

Sharon looked worried, though. She was more normal, like me. Also, we were both twelve. Ax was thirteen and more confident.

Miss Spice pulled down her wall map of the world. It was an old-fashioned map like some classrooms still use. She pointed to an island near Australia.

"New Guinea," she said. "Second largest island in the world, after Greenland. And without question one of the wildest places left on the planet."

I was stunned. "We're going there?"

She nodded grimly. "I'm afraid so."

"I've read about it," Sharon said, suddenly excited. "They've got all kinds of neat animals." She was as crazy about wildlife as Ax was about karate.

"Wait a minute," I said, shaking my head as I thought of Roy and Pam Williams and the book I'd recently read. "We can't be going there. We just can't be."

"Why not?" Ax said.

I sat back in my chair. "Never mind. It's just too weird."

Miss Spice shrugged. "Anyway, yes, you're right, Sharon. They have fascinating examples of wildlife there. And one of the most unusual is the bird of paradise. Ever heard of it?"

We shook our heads.

"Some call it the most beautiful bird in the world," Miss Spice said. "They're not that big— about the size of pigeons, maybe—but their colors are just electric."

She handed us a book. Sharon opened it and Ax and I stared. Wow! The birds had colors like stoplight red, satin purple, mustard yellow, pool table green, and dragonfly tail blue.

"Most species are found in New Guinea," Miss Spice said. "But they're very rare. They've been hunted for years for those feathers, for women's hats and clothing. But now hunting them is outlawed."

"I know! Somebody's killing them and you want us to catch him," Ax guessed.

"Exactly," Miss Spice said. "His name is Edward Miller, but he's known as Muruk."

"Muruk! I know that word," I said, remembering it from the Williams' book. "It's pidgin for cassowary."

They stared at me.

"That's right, Eric, but how could you possibly have known that?" Miss Spice said.

"Yes, and what's pidgin and cassowary?" Ax said.

"You guys won't believe all this," I said. "A missionary from New Guinea spoke at our church a couple weeks ago. He wrote a book, and I read it. Pidgin is the language most people speak there. Similar to English. Muruk is the pidgin word for cassowary, which is a giant bird that can kill people."

"Cool!" Ax said.

I nodded. "It rips your guts out with its claws. The missionary got attacked and barely survived."

"Eric, that's incredible," Miss Spice said.

"But it's true! It says so in the book."

"No, I mean that you met this missionary. It's uncanny."

"So what's our assignment?" Ax prompted.

"Just a minute. Eric, tell me more about this missionary," Miss Spice said.

"Well, his name is Roy Williams, and his wife is named Pam. They live in the town of Wewak. They've had all kinds of jungle adventures, like being chased by cannibals. Oh, and Ax, he knows some kenpo, a type of karate."

"I'm familiar with it," Ax said, nodding.

"This is just too strange," Miss Spice said, shaking her head. "This could be the answer to my prayer."

"What do you mean?" Sharon asked.

Miss Spice returned to her desk. "Here's my

problem. We've sent adult agents after Muruk before. One agent even got wounded by a shotgun blast in the jungle, though we can't prove Muruk did it. Usually, though, his contacts warn him when a stranger arrives and he disappears into the jungle. That's why I thought of you kids. I figured you wouldn't seem as threatening. But I can't very well send you into the New Guinea bush without an adult. Not only is it too dangerous, it would seem highly unusual for three kids to be traveling on their own over there. What I need is an experienced adult to go with you but who won't attract any attention."

"Yeah." I nodded. "Like somebody who already lives there."

"Exactly," she said. "And you want to know something really strange?" She lowered her voice. "Muruk lives in Wewak."

3

"This has got to be the hand of God," Miss Spice said. "You know what they say, God works in mysterious ways, his wonders to perform."

"Yeah, quite a coincidence," I said.

Miss Spice smiled. "Call it what you will, all I know is I've been praying for God to help me find a solution. Eric, how do I get in touch with the Williamses?"

"My parents should know."

She handed me the phone. "Find out, please."

I called Dad at work. He said the Williamses had gone on to another state on their fund-raising tour. He said he would ask the church secretary how to get in touch with them.

"That's good," said Miss Spice. "I'll call him. If

things go the way I hope, the Williamses can give us a hand. We'll pay them well, and the money will help their mission work."

"But do we really need an adult?" Ax said. "We usually do this stuff on our own."

"New Guinea is a dangerous place," Miss Spice said.

"Yeah, cannibals," I said.

"There is a history of cannibalism, but that's not what concerns me," she said. "The people are not as primitive as they used to be. They're not in the Stone Age anymore. But the jungle is a difficult and dangerous place, and Muruk is not one to be trifled with."

"So what's the plan?" Ax said. "I mean, assuming the Williamses agree to help?"

Miss Spice nodded. "If they agree, you three will use their house as your headquarters. I'll need you to find Muruk and put him under surveillance. As soon as you do, call our agent in Port Moresby; that's the capital. Since you'll have Muruk's location pinpointed, my hope would be that the agent can fly in and make the arrest—with the help of local government officials, of course."

"What if Muruk is off hunting?"

"Good question. Then you'll need to get Roy Williams to help you track him down."

"And then what?" I asked.

"Arrest him. That may be tricky, which is why I want an adult along."

"Won't we need some kind of evidence, like bird of paradise feathers?" Sharon asked.

"The chances are, if you find Muruk, you'll find contraband feathers. The hard part is going to be finding him. He's as elusive as the cassowary he's named after."

The phone rang. It was my dad, with a number where the Williamses could be reached. Miss Spice called but they were out. She agreed to try again later.

"In the meantime, there's much for you to do," she told us. She reached into her desk and pulled out three bottles of pills. "Malaria medicine. Take one pill today and one every week. You have to start taking them two weeks before you go."

She got us some water and we swallowed. The pill tasted incredibly bitter even for the short time it was in my mouth.

"I'm sorry I forgot snacks," Miss Spice said as we gulped glasses of water. "I've been so worried about this assignment I haven't been thinking straight."

"So we'll leave in two weeks?" Ax asked.

"Right. Which gives you time for this." Miss Spice reached into her desk and pulled out three floppy green books and a pair of cassette tapes.

"A course in pidgin. I want you to study it together for half an hour every night. If you practice with each other you'll learn the language much more quickly."

"That sounds like homework!" I protested.

"Actually, it's fun," she said. "I've learned a little myself. *Mi laikim yupela planti tumas.*"

We giggled. "What does that mean?" Sharon asked.

"Me like you fellows plenty too-much. In other words, I like you guys a lot." Miss Spice smiled. "But you may not like me after you hear the next thing I want you to do."

"Uh-oh," I said.

"I've got three backpacks loaded with heavy weights. Every afternoon at two o'clock my driver will take you to the city stadium to hike up and down the steps for one hour."

"What!" I howled.

"Piece of cake," said Ax, who worked out all the time anyway.

"But those steps are steep," I said. "And that's the hottest part of the day!"

"Exactly," Miss Spice said. "In New Guinea you may be hiking up steep mountains with heavy packs in tropical temperatures. Believe me, you'll thank me for this later."

"It sounds hard, but I'm willing if it will help the birds of paradise," Sharon said.

"But what if the Williamses won't help us?" I said, looking for a way out.

"Oh, they will," Miss Spice said. "I have faith."

She was right about the missionaries. She got in touch with them that night. Not wanting to discuss secret details on the phone, Miss Spice flew out to see the Williamses the next day.

When she got back, she said Roy and Pam were eager to help.

"They remembered you," Miss Spice told me over the phone. "Pam wasn't totally surprised when I told her you worked for us. She said she thought there was more to you than met the eye."

Hey! She was even cooler than I thought.

The Williamses were planning to return to New Guinea in a week, so they would be waiting for us when we arrived.

For the next two weeks, Ax, Sharon, and I practiced pidgin, hiked at the stadium, and read up on New Guinea. Our parents were actually excited about the assignment. Ax and Sharon's folks were glad their kids would be getting to see some exotic wildlife up close. Mine were thrilled because I'd be working with missionaries supported by our own church. Dad even told my Sunday school teacher I was going—he didn't say why, of course—since the man had visited there himself once. The teacher suggested one of us kids hold onto all the passports—that's the way church groups do it—so after we boarded the plane, Sharon and I gave ours to Ax.

As the plane lifted off on its long journey west, my hands were sweaty. Miss Spice had called this our most dangerous mission yet. Considering our past adventures, I had good reason to be nervous.

4

We changed planes in Honolulu in the middle of the night. At dawn we switched again on the island of Guam. We had been there on an earlier adventure about the secret of Lizard Island, but I was too tired to think about it. I hadn't slept much at all—just couldn't get comfortable on the plane.

We left Guam and continued flying over the Pacific Ocean. We had flown over it all night and still had hours to go! That was a lot of water—and a lot of miles between us and home.

About twenty hours after leaving home, we saw the island of New Guinea rising out of the sea. There was a flat stretch of scummy-looking swamp backed by huge jungle-covered mountains stretching into the distance. There were no roads, no towns, just forest and grassland.

"Now I see why Miss Spice was worried," I told my friends, who leaned over to stare out my window.

"It looks spooky, all right," Ax said. "So big."

"If we get lost down there, we can't just follow a compass course to the nearest road," Sharon said.

We flew for quite a while over this seemingly endless island, and the only signs of humans we saw were thatched huts and gardens here and there. At midday we finally came to a city scattered along the coast. The plane angled down. Must be Port Moresby, I figured, the capital.

As we came in for a landing, I felt woozy; I guess from lack of sleep. The plane taxied to a halt and the engine died. In moments it was steaming hot inside. All the passengers reached for their luggage, but no one opened the door.

"What are they waiting for?" Sharon said, frowning.

"Uh, you guys, I'd better make a quick trip to the bathroom," Ax said.

"Wait! Our passports," I said. "We might need them."

"Oh yeah." He tossed them to us and vanished down the aisle.

Then a stewardess appeared. "Children first," she said as someone opened the cabin door. She pointed to Sharon and me. "Come on."

"But my brother," Sharon began.

"Come on, he can catch up," I said. "It's hot in here."

We grabbed our flight bags and headed out, down the steps into blinding sunshine. It felt like the hottest, muggiest summer day back home, only worse. Other passengers crowded behind us as we walked across the pavement toward a big metal building.

"Should we wait out here for Ax?" Sharon asked, glancing back anxiously.

"Let's hurry up so we won't have to stand in line," I said. "Maybe it'll be cooler inside."

It wasn't. The big building was not air-conditioned, and sweat began to trickle down my face. Three men stood at counters waiting to check our papers. Sharon went first.

A bored man in uniform flipped through her passport, stamping it here and there, and mumbled some questions I didn't hear. Finally he nodded and gave her the passport. She went through a turnstile.

"I'm going to find a fountain," she told me, and went down a hall and around a corner.

I handed the man my passport. He flipped it open.

"Your name?"

"Eric Sterling."

He glanced at the passport, then at me, then back at the passport. "Tell me again your name?"

"Eric Sterling, sir."

The man shook his head. "You try to fool me, no? You are not Eric Sterling." He held up the passport—and I saw Ax's photo! He'd given me the wrong passport! And since Ax's name is Erik Stirling, the guard obviously thought I was an impostor.

He motioned to a soldier standing by the wall. The man unshouldered his rifle and hurried over.

"Wait! You don't understand!" I spun around to look for Ax but saw only a wall of impatient passengers. "Ax! Hey, Ax!" My words could barely be heard over their voices.

Sharon was still gone. I faced the official and tried to appear calm.

"I'm not *that* Erik Stirling," I explained. "That passport belongs to my friend Erik. He's Erik with a *k*, you see, and I'm Eric with a *c*, okay? I mean, he's Ax, that's his nickname, and I'm just plain Eric, and I've got his passport by mistake ..."

The man stared at me with a frown. "Take him," he told the soldier. "The colonel will deal with him later, no?"

The soldier grabbed my arm.

"No, wait," I pleaded as he dragged me to a closed door. "Ax! Sharon!" I yelled.

The soldier opened the door, shoved me in, and slammed it behind me, locking it. I was in a tiny room with a table and two chairs. On the table were a few scattered papers and an ash tray with several

cigarette butts. The room reminded me of the inter-
rogation room in TV police shows.

Great! I was about to be questioned, maybe tor-
tured, then tossed in a New Guinea jail.

Fine way to start an assignment, no?

5

Before long the door opened again and Ax tumbled in. The door clicked behind him.

"Ax! What are you doing in here?"

"I could ask you the same thing," he said, brushing his shirt angrily.

"But surely the official realized what happened."

"Which line were you in?"

"The one on the far side," I said.

He nodded. "I was at the nearest. We had different guys."

"Does Sharon even know we're in here?"

"I haven't seen her," Ax said. "Here, give me my passport. Here's yours. And next time you see your Sunday school teacher, tell him thanks for nothing."

"It wasn't his fault you got them mixed up."

"Oh, I see. So I'm the one to blame."

"No, I mean—well, we just got in too big a hurry," I said. No need for *us* to fight.

Just then the door opened and a scowling officer came in wearing a pistol. The colonel!

"What is the problem here?" he demanded.

"A simple mix-up, sir," Ax said. "We're both named Eric Sterling, only we spell our names differently."

"He accidentally handed me my passport and he kept mine," I added.

"Let me see." He took our passports impatiently, opened them, examined the photos, and compared them to our faces. "How do I know you're not spies?" he said suspiciously.

Ax and I glanced at each other. I cleared my throat. "Well, uh . . ."

The man smiled. Then he chuckled. Then he began to laugh. "I'm making a joke," he said between chortles. "Anyone can see *you* two are no secret agents."

Ax scowled. "What? Wait just a minute! How do you *know* we're not secret agents?"

I elbowed him. What was he trying to do, get us shot?

The official, still laughing, pointed at me. "You expect me to believe *this* little boy is a spy?"

"Hey!" I protested. "What makes you so sure, anyway?"

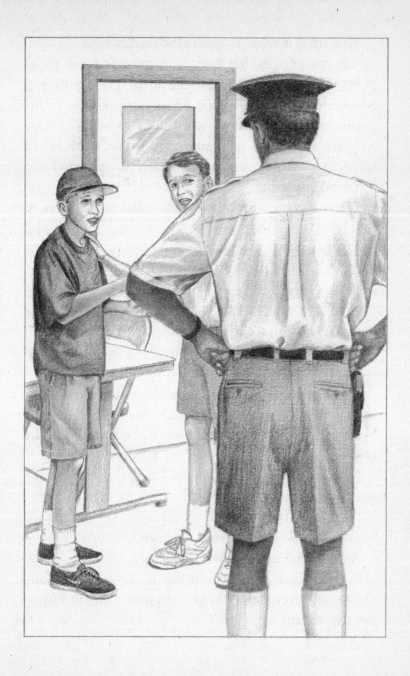

This time it was Ax who elbowed me.

The man wiped his eyes, then stamped our passports. He handed Ax his passport. "Here you are, Mr. James Bond, Jr." Then he gave me mine. "And you—how do you say—Mr. Pink Panther?"

"Very funny!" I said angrily. I was just about to tell him who we *really* were when Ax grabbed my arm and pulled me to the door.

"Thank you, sir," he said. "Thank you very much."

The man let us out. "Give my regards to the head of the CIA," he said, still chuckling as we walked away.

"What a smart alec," I muttered as we got our backpacks from a cargo rack.

"Just be glad he didn't really think we were spies," Ax said, but I could tell he felt insulted too.

We went to a line where customs officials looked through people's baggage. I felt almost angry when they just waved us through—as if they, too, thought we were too young to be secret agents!

"Where have you two been?" asked Sharon, who was waiting for us.

"We got our passports mixed up," Ax said.

"We almost got arrested as spies," I said.

Ax glanced at me. "Yeah. *Almost*."

"We need to go to the ticket office and find out about our flight to Wewak," Sharon told us impatiently. "Come on, guys."

We walked down a long hall into the lobby, which was open to the parking lot. My clothes were damp with sweat.

All around people bustled. The New Guineans were dressed in modern clothes, and I remembered Miss Spice saying they weren't in the Stone Age anymore. No one paid us much attention.

At the ticket counter we learned that our plane was supposed to leave in two hours, so we sprawled out on hard plastic chairs to wait.

"Man, I can't believe how tired I am," I said.

"It's jet lag," Sharon explained. "New Guinea is sixteen hours ahead of home because of all the time zones."

"That means our bodies think it's bedtime," Ax said.

"But it's the middle of the day!" I said. "No wonder I feel so weird."

"Yeah, but it doesn't explain why you *look* so weird," Ax said with a grin.

"Very funny." I slouched down in my seat, closed my eyes, and tried to nap. No luck.

Finally it was time to board the plane. This one was smaller than the jet that had brought us from Guam. It had four propellers.

We took off and soon were flying over the same type of wild and rugged landscape we'd seen coming in. After crossing lots of jungly mountains, we saw a wide plain with a curvy river.

"Is that the Sepik?" Sharon asked.

"Probably," I said.

"That's where they used to have headhunters," Ax said.

"Wonderful," I muttered.

It was late afternoon when we landed at Wewak, a small town on the north coast. As we staggered off the plane into blasting heat, I saw palm trees and thunderclouds and New Guineans staring curiously. I felt far from home and certainly not up to any jungle adventures.

Then I saw Pam Williams. She was smiling as we approached the small terminal.

"Eric," she said, holding out her arms. She hugged me like we were family. "This must be Sharon and Ax." She embraced them too. "I know how tired you must be. Roy is at the house. Come on and we'll get you cleaned up and fed."

6

The Williamses lived in a small white house on stilts, with a metal roof. Pam parked their jeep under the house and we climbed the steps to the front porch. The walls were mostly screen with heavy iron bars across them.

Roy was in the kitchen frying potatoes. "Welcome!" he said with a grin as Pam introduced him to Ax and Sharon. On the counter by the stove, a mound of home fries lay heaped on newspapers. I suddenly felt hungry.

"We're going to eat a little early so we can run over to Timbunke and pick up a shotgun," Roy told us.

"Shotgun?" I asked. "What for?"

He glanced at his wife. "You haven't told them?"

31

She shook her head. "Haven't had time, sweetie."

"We're leaving tomorrow," Roy said. "Got a report that Muruk was at Yellow River. That's way up the Sepik. I thought it would be wise to take a gun. We might have to go in the bush."

"They may not feel up to riding to Timbunke tonight," Pam said. "It's a long way. In fact, I'm not convinced it's safe."

"It's been months since anybody was robbed," Roy said, flipping potatoes in the skillet.

"Yes, but you never know when they'll try again," she said as she set the table.

"Did somebody say robbed?" Sharon said.

"Yeah. You kids don't have to go if you don't want to," Roy said. "I'm sure you're worn out after your trip."

"I want to go," Ax said.

"Sharon, why don't you stay here and help me pack?" Pam suggested. "You can too, Eric, if you like."

I shrugged. "I'll go."

"All right!" Ax said.

When Pam finished setting the table she showed us to our rooms. Sharon got the guest room, which had a bed, while Ax and I would have to camp in the office.

By the time we stowed our stuff and finished supper it was dark outside. We were just about to get up from the table when something clanged on the metal roof.

"Is that hail?" Sharon said.

It clanged again.

"It's Saturday night," Roy said. "People get drunk and throw rocks sometimes."

"You mean they're throwing rocks at the house?" Ax asked. "Let's go stop them!"

Pam smiled. "They're harmless drunks, most likely. Leave them alone and they'll go on their way."

"Yeah, but still," Ax said.

"Happens all the time," Roy said, clearing away dishes. "You boys about ready?"

"Is it safe to leave Pam and Sharon alone?" I asked. "I mean, with the drunks and all?"

"Sure. We're used to it," Roy said.

I was full of bad feelings as we climbed into the jeep. I wished I was home in my own bed, curled up for a long night's sleep. Instead I was in a hostile country where people threw stones and robbed travelers.

I slid into the back of the open-topped jeep while Ax took the front. Off we went into the blackness. The streets in town weren't great, but they were even worse in the countryside. Roy drove fast, and I had to grip the roll bar to keep from flying off my seat. Our route twisted, turned, rose, and fell. And Roy yanked the jeep from one side to another to dodge potholes. It was so dark I couldn't tell anything about our surroundings. All I could see was the gravel track in the headlights.

We topped a hill and suddenly the road seemed to disappear. Roy skidded to a halt at the bottom.

"What on earth?" Roy said.

As we eased forward, the headlights shone on a broad sheet of water.

"Flooded," he said. "Well, here goes."

He drove the vehicle into the river. I couldn't see the far side. The water lapped at the floorboards but didn't quite come inside. Steam rose from underneath.

"Any deeper we'll have to stop," Roy said.

Then we saw the far bank. The water got shallower, and we were out, streams running off the knobby tires.

"Thank you, Lord," Roy said, but he didn't sound worried. My knuckles were white from holding on.

Ax turned around and grinned. "Cool, huh?"

"Sure."

Roy slammed on the brakes.

"What is it now?" I said.

Up ahead, blocking the road, stood a row of oil drums.

"Bad news, boys," Roy said. "It looks like Pam was right after all."

Half a dozen men stepped out of the darkness holding clubs, spears, and machetes.

7

Roy slammed the jeep into reverse, but there was nowhere to turn around. The narrow road lay between steep banks. Behind us was the river. The robbers had chosen their spot well.

"Maybe I can talk them out of it," Roy said.

"I'll talk them out of it," Ax said angrily, and leaped out of the jeep with a karate shout. He took a fighting position, fists up, feet apart.

Roy shook his head. "I wish he hadn't done that."

The men, dressed in ragged clothes, appeared drunk and mad. Like a lot of the New Guineans we'd seen, they weren't that big, but they looked strong. One of them moved toward Ax and jabbed a spear straight at him.

Ax stepped to the side, grabbed the shaft, and kicked the man in the ribs. He crumpled and fell, leaving Ax with the spear.

"Not bad," Roy muttered, climbing out. Then he stepped into a fighting position. Kenpo!

The gang attacked. It all happened so fast I could hardly move. Two guys came at Ax, one with a machete and one with a club. Using the spear like a staff, Ax knocked one man's legs out from under him. Then he did an upward block with the spear to ward off a club strike. Next he jabbed the blunt end into his attacker's chest. I could hear the man's breath go out with a *whoosh* as he doubled over.

Meanwhile Roy grabbed one man's hand and twisted it somehow so the guy flipped over and landed on his back. Then he kicked another guy's leg and slammed him to the ground; the man landed with a grunt.

Five men down—where was the sixth?

A shadow appeared beside me as the sixth man swung a club at my head! I ducked and it slammed into the seat back. Reaching for anything I could find on the floor, I came up with a set of battery jumper cables. Some weapon! But it was all I had, so I slung it around at the guy's face. The metal part slashed him across the forehead, and blood poured into his eyes. He put his hands to his face and stumbled backward, then tripped and landed on his back.

"Good job, guys," Roy said. "I hate to do this sort

of thing, but sometimes you don't have much choice."

The men lay around us, groaning.

"Let's move these barrels, Eric," Roy said. "Ax, you keep an eye on our friends here."

The barrels were heavy—filled with concrete! We rolled them out of the way. When we finished, the men were getting to their feet but did not show any fight.

"They're just drunk," Roy said. Then he spoke loudly. *"Yupela makem wanem? Bilong wanem yu traim dispela? Em i nogut tru. Nau harim!"* (What are you fellows doing? Why did you try this? It's no good. Now listen!)

The men looked up at him, shame-faced.

"Yupela savvy sios bilong Markun?" Roy asked. (Do you know the church at Markun?)

Two or three nodded. One man cleared his throat. *"Mipela savvy,"* he replied in a deep voice. (We know it.)

"Sunday long tenpela kilok mi laik yupela kam long dispela sios na pretim Jisas forgivim yupela. Yu savvy?" (Sunday at ten o'clock I want you fellows to come to this church and pray to Jesus to forgive you. Understand?)

They nodded.

"Orait, nau yu go lon ghaus bilong yupela. Nogut yu makem dispela kain samting gen." (All right, now go home. Don't try this kind of thing again.)

They took their weapons and stumbled into the darkness.

"I don't believe it," Ax said. "You mean you just invited them to church? Why not call the police?"

Roy laughed. "What police? We're in the bush, lad. You just have to make do. Besides, church would do them more good than jail."

Ax shrugged. "You may be right. But do you think they'll come?"

"Maybe not this Sunday, but who knows? You plant a seed and it sprouts in its own time." He cranked the jeep and we got under way. "By the way, you're good. What style do you practice?"

"Tang Soo Do. It's a Korean style. You do kenpo, right?"

"Right. It has elements of kung fu and karate."

"It sure seemed to work," I said.

"Well, I don't know that much, really," Roy said. "I haven't taken lessons since I was in college. I just practice the basics. It's a good way to stay in shape, plus it comes in handy for self-defense, as you can see."

Ax nodded vigorously. "The basics, that's all you need. My instructor says that the more advanced you are, the fewer techniques you actually use. Some masters only use one or two techniques because they're so good at them."

"Eric, you looked pretty good back there, yourself," Roy said.

"Yeah," Ax said. "What'd you hit that guy with, a crowbar?"

"Jumper cables. I've spent years practicing that technique," I joked.

They laughed. "Well, it did the trick," Roy said. "That's all that matters. Like I said, I hate violence. On the other hand, I'm not going to stand by and let somebody hurt you guys. Incidentally, Ax, next time don't be so quick to fight. It's possible I could have talked those guys out of it. I've done it before."

"Yes sir," he said.

I just hoped there wouldn't be a next time.

8

At Timbunke Roy borrowed a shotgun and some old-timey paper shells from a friend. On the long drive back I dozed despite the rough road.

It was late when we got in. Pam and Sharon had gone to bed. Ax and I climbed into our sleeping bags on the office floor, and it seemed like I had just fallen asleep when Pam woke us for breakfast.

"We're going to church at Markun this morning," she said. "This afternoon we'll fly to Yellow River."

We ate cold cereal, then drove to a village on a dirt road full of potholes. Roy had to put the jeep in four-wheel drive. The sun was hot and blinding even this early in the morning.

"We started this church here," Pam said as we

got out at the edge of a group of huts among banana and palm trees. "It's still in its infancy."

"We meet under this tarp," Roy said, pointing to a bright blue folded sheet of plastic in the back. "If you guys get it I'll carry the poles."

Ax and I lifted the heavy tarp, and we all walked to the center of the village. People greeted us with smiles and friendly words. The air smelled of wood smoke, and pigs grunted under the raised houses.

A smiling man came out to welcome us.

"Kids, this is Lester," Roy said. "He's our chief elder here."

Lester had very dark skin and kindly eyes. He looked about Roy's age. He wore khaki pants, a white shirt, and flip-flops.

"Welcome to Markun," he said. "Let me help you with the tent."

As we raised the tarp, somebody banged a metal pipe against a butane tank, like a church bell, and people began to wander over. Women wore long wraparound skirts and T-shirts, and many carried babies. Men wore slacks or shorts. Nobody was dressed up by American standards.

About twenty people sat on the ground, while others watched from the houses. Lester led the group in pidgin hymns whose tunes sounded familiar. After prayer and announcements, Roy began to preach.

He told us to turn our Bibles to Psalm 91. He was

reading in pidgin, but I could follow along in my own Bible. I didn't pay close attention at first, but then some verses made me listen up.

"You will not fear the terror of night, nor the arrow that flies by day, nor the pestilence that stalks in the darkness. No harm will befall you, no disaster will come near your tent."

Terror at night? Arrows by day? It sounded like the writer was talking about New Guinea.

I shuddered when I remembered our fight with the robbers. It was like a bad dream. And after so little sleep, I still felt shaky.

I remembered Roy's invitation to the men. I looked around the congregation. If any of them had come, I didn't recognize them. I didn't really think they would anyway. But maybe it was like Roy said, the "seed" would sprout someday and they would show up and listen.

After church, Lester joined us at the jeep, carrying a knapsack.

"He's going with us to Yellow River," Roy explained as Lester squeezed in the back with us kids. "He's a good man to have along in the bush."

Lester grinned. "I was raised on the Sepik."

"He's an old crocodile hunter," Pam said. "He ought to be a match for Muruk."

Lester held out his right forearm, and we saw a long, jagged scar.

"*Pukpuk*," he said. "Crocodile."

"Wow!" Ax said. "What happened?"

"One day I was walking down to the canoes. A *pukpuk* was lying there and I didn't see him. He looked just like a canoe. He jumped and grabbed my arm."

Sharon examined the row of raised, purplish welts. "Then what happened?" she said.

"My older brother was there. He jammed a spear right into the *pukpuk's* eye. Into the brain. That's the only way he would let go."

"How long was he?" I asked.

Lester shrugged. "Three meters or so."

"That's, like, ten feet," Ax said. "Man!"

"Now I am very careful when I go around the water," Lester said with a grin.

After a quick lunch, we put our backpacks in the jeep and drove to the airport. We carried the packs to a small single-prop plane.

"Where's the pilot?" Ax asked.

"You're looking at him," Roy said with a smile.

"I didn't know you could fly," I said. "I read your book, by the way. It was good."

"Thanks. The book ended where I decided to become a missionary. I figured knowing how to fly would come in handy here in New Guinea, since there aren't many roads. So Pam and I went back to the States and I got my pilot's license while going to seminary."

We loaded our gear in the belly of the aircraft and

climbed inside. It was a six-seater. I sat in the rear with Lester.

"Here's a map," Pam said. She unfolded it in Ax and Sharon's laps so we could all see. It was big and detailed.

Rivers and streams spread out like a spiderweb. There were few roads or towns, just villages with strange names like Yaru, Akwom, and Nami.

"Jungle and swamp," Lester said, tapping the map at Yellow River. "The people here are very primitive."

"Nomads," Pam added. "Hunters and gatherers."

"We've read about those in social studies," Sharon said.

"Everybody buckled in and ready?" Roy called.

"Ready back here," Lester replied.

Pam folded the map and turned to the front.

"All right," Roy said, flipping switches. "Here we go."

9

We flew over a not-too-high mountain range, and then over flat jungle and swamp. After a while I saw a brown river way off to the left.

"Sepik," Lester said.

Then we flew over a creek and I saw a few metal roofs and several thatched ones. We came in for a landing on a grass airstrip. When the motor stopped we climbed out into scorching heat. Nobody was around.

"Welcome to Yellow River," Roy said, brushing a fly away from his face. "Not the most happenin' place on earth."

We hoisted our packs and walked up a path.

"Are there any missionaries here?" Sharon asked.

"There's a nurse," Pam said. "Miss Sherry, from New Zealand. She's about to retire, though, and there's no one to replace her."

"You guys!" Ax hissed. "Check this out!"

Coming down the trail toward us was a man followed by a woman carrying a child. At first glance I thought the man was stark naked. He was skinny and brown with bushy gray hair and a shell necklace. Then I saw he did have something on: a pointed brown gourd, long and skinny, held up by a cord around the waist. That was all.

"Don't look, Sharon," Ax whispered.

Pam laughed. "You'd better get used to it."

The woman wore a wraparound skirt and nothing else. Her chest was covered with some kind of scaly skin disease. The baby she carried was naked, and had the same skin disease on its mouth and cheeks. It probably caught it from suckling its mother.

"Now *you* don't look," Sharon told Ax.

The family stepped aside to let us pass.

"*Apinun tru*," Roy said. (Good afternoon.)

The man grinned, showing teeth that were almost black. His mouth was stuffed with something like chewing tobacco. "*Apinun tru*," he said. He leaned over and spat out a big red glob.

"Gross," Ax whispered.

"That's *buai*," Lester explained. "Betel nut."

The woman smiled but kept her eyes on the ground as we passed.

"Does everybody around here dress like that?" I asked.

"No," Roy said. "That's traditional attire. A lot of people wear clothes donated by missionaries. But they don't have the same notions of decency that we do. Like Pam said, you'd better get used to it."

"What's that *buai* stuff?" Ax asked.

"The nut of the betel palm tree," Pam said. "It has a slightly narcotic effect. Everybody chews it."

"I saw people chewing it at Wewak," I said. "I assumed it was chewing tobacco."

"Man, when he spit that out, I thought it was blood," Ax said.

"It's a bad habit," Roy said as we approached a gray wooden house with a metal roof. He knocked on the door and a short, white-haired lady appeared.

"Why, Roy and Pam! What a surprise! Come on in," she said, obviously startled.

"I'm sorry I didn't radio," Roy said as we entered the cool, dark house. "I had good reason not to, though."

Miss Sherry frowned. "A problem? But first, introduce me to your friends."

"This is Ax, Sharon, and Eric. They're visiting from the States," Pam said. "You may have met Lester at Markun."

"Oh yes, of course. So glad to see you all. Let me get you something to drink." Miss Sherry's accent sounded like Australian accents I'd heard on TV, but a little different.

47

She poured us glasses of fruit drink. We sat at a table and sipped.

"Now, tell me all about it," the nurse said.

"We're looking for Muruk—Edward Miller," Roy said. "But we don't want him to know we're looking for him."

Miss Sherry frowned. "The law's finally closing in on him, and you're helping out. Is that it?"

"How did you know?" Pam asked.

Miss Sherry shrugged. "Everybody knows he's a poacher, one of the worst. I assumed it was a matter of time till the law caught up with him. But he's too smart to be caught by police. So they got a local to help."

"I just hope he doesn't figure it out so easily," Roy said.

"He's not here anyway. He left a couple weeks ago. Stopped by to get some medicine, then said he was going to Tipas, on the Sepik. From there, who knows? He keeps his plans to himself."

"That's what, eight miles or so from here?" Roy asked.

She nodded. "Half a day's walk if you go fast."

"Well, it's too late to go today," he said, glancing at his watch. "We'll hike over first thing in the morning. Maybe we can catch up with him, or at least find out where he went."

"Fine. I know you must be tired," Miss Sherry said. "I'll get dinner started."

10

Ax and I shared a guest room that had twin beds and big screened windows. Rain beat on the metal roof all night.

For breakfast we all had toast, jam, and hot tea. We put on our packs, thanked Miss Sherry, and set out down the trail to Tipas. The rain was over and the morning sun was hot and steamy.

We passed several thatched huts. They all looked empty.

"Where is everybody?" Ax asked. "This seems like a ghost town."

"They're out collecting *tons*," Lester said.

"What's that?"

"A wild jungle fruit. Now is when they're ripe."

The trail crossed a grassy field and came to Yellow River, a mud-brown creek with a few huts on the far side. Roy shouted, and a man and a boy appeared and paddled a dugout canoe to us.

"There used to be a wooden bridge here," Roy said. "Flood washed it out."

We climbed into the long, skinny canoe. The boatman wore shorts and chewed betel nut. He grinned and chattered, but I couldn't understand him. The boy paddled us across, and we climbed a steep dirt bank. Then we were on the trail again.

"Believe it or not, this used to be a road," Roy said as we hiked through deep grass with jungle on either side. "Some people flew in a whole tractor in pieces and put it together. They built a bridge and pushed a road out to the Sepik. But the bridge washed out and the tractor broke down and the weeds grew up." He shook his head. "That's the bush for you."

The muddy trail sucked at our ankles, making it hard to walk. Ax and Sharon, who wore shorts, complained that the sharp grass was cutting their legs. Whenever we came to a creek we had to walk across on logs, which was scary. The air was hot and muggy. We swigged from canteens but stayed thirsty. Whenever we stopped, flies landed on our faces.

Sometimes we heard shouts and ax blows far out in the jungle. Lester said that was people gathering *tons*.

It took several hours to reach Tipas, which was

just a few huts on the bank of the Sepik. At least there was a breeze there, blowing off the wide brown river. On the far side, in the distance, stood a range of blue mountains.

We stopped outside a hut.

"*Morning,*" Roy called. "*Yupela stap gut?*" (Good morning. How are you?)

No one stirred. A big black hog wandered over, sniffing us. It brushed its snout against my pants leg.

"Get back!" I commanded.

The hog snorted and shoved me with its head. I realized it had no fear of me—and it was bigger than I! This wasn't some tame farm pig. It was a beast! A shiver went through me.

Lester scratched the creature's back gently, talking to it in a soothing tone. The hog's angry grunts became calmer.

"I'll bet that's why the houses are on stilts," Ax said. "To keep the hogs out."

The beast wandered off, searching for something to eat. I was glad it hadn't picked me for its dinner.

"*Morning!*" Roy repeated. "*Mipela laik toktok lik-lik.*" (We want to talk a little.)

Slowly someone began shuffling around inside, and an old, shriveled-up man walked out onto the porch. Around his neck was a string from which dangled teeth and weird furry animal parts. He wore only a loincloth of thick, bunchy grass. His mouth was stuffed with *buai*, and his eyes were red and wicked. He glanced at us, and for some reason his gaze fastened on me. I felt another shiver go through me. Was he mad because I was rude to his hog?

Then he raised his hand, and I saw that he was holding a bone. He pointed it at me and began to mumble. As he spoke, a stream of bright red ran down his jaw.

"What's he saying?" Roy muttered to Lester.

"I don't know. It's in his own language."

"Why is he pointing at Eric?"

"I think he's some kind of sorcerer," Lester said nervously.

Their voices faded as the old man's evil gaze bored into me. His words hummed around me like bees. The bone was aimed straight at my head, like a pistol. My skin tingled and my head began to throb.

"Enough of that!" Roy said.

The sorcerer continued to mumble and drool blood-colored spit.

"I said enough!" Roy said. Then he pointed at the man. "In the name of Jesus Christ, I tell you to be quiet."

"Roy, you're speaking English," Pam whispered. "You need to say it in pidgin."

"He understood me all right," Roy said.

The sorcerer dropped his hand and quit mumbling. He blinked his mean, bloodshot eyes, as if

he'd been in a trance. Then he hobbled back into the shadows of the hut.

Pam shuddered. "I don't like this place, Roy."

Lester nodded. "Evil spirits here."

"Ah, superstition," Roy said. He glanced around. "But I don't see any sign of Muruk. It looks like we're too late."

They kept talking, but I lost interest. My head hurt, and I felt weak. I squatted down to rest.

"You okay, big guy?" Ax asked.

"I don't feel so good."

"The sorcerer," Lester said. "He has cast a spell."

"Don't be ridiculous!" Roy snapped. "And don't fill his head with those ideas, Lester."

Lester shrugged. "I have seen it happen before."

"Let's go back, Roy," Pam pleaded. "It's obvious Muruk isn't here."

Roy sighed. "I don't like to give up so soon, but I guess you're right." He cast one last angry look at the hut. "Come on," he said. "Let's go."

11

"Here, I'll take your pack," Lester offered.

I was staggering and we hadn't gone a mile.

"I'll carry it," I said.

"Mine is light. I can carry yours easily," he insisted.

"Why don't you let him?" Pam urged. "You don't want to make yourself sick."

So I gave Lester my pack, which helped.

On the trail we met a man and a boy carrying string bags full of *tons*. They stopped and offered us some. I tried one, a fruit the size of a plum and just as sweet. It made me feel a little better. I sat on a log while Roy and Lester asked about Muruk.

Just the mention of his name made the man

nervous. He replied in a high-pitched, excited voice. The boy, too, looked scared.

"What did you find out?" Ax asked when the man and boy had left.

Roy shook his head. "They said Muruk crossed the Sepik on a long hunt into the mountains. No way to catch up with him now."

Normally I would have been disappointed, but right now I felt too sick to care. As we resumed hiking, I just got worse. My legs ached, my head swam. By the time we got to Miss Sherry's house, all I wanted to do was lie down.

Pam put me to bed and brought me a tall glass of fruit juice. Then she went to get Miss Sherry, who was working at the clinic. Soon the white-haired nurse sat at my side, and everybody stood around her, watching.

She put her hand on my forehead. "Got a touch of fever," she said. "Have you been taking your malaria medicine?"

"Yes, ma'am."

She stuck a thermometer in my mouth. "There's a hundred kinds of fever out here," she said. "We don't know half of them."

"It's more than fever," Lester said. "It's the spell."

"Lester!" Roy said with a frown.

"What spell?" Miss Sherry asked.

"Oh, some would-be sorcerer tried to throw a scare into the boy with the usual mumbo-jumbo," Roy said. "Lester here still believes in that stuff."

"A lot of people do, Roy," Pam said. "A lot of missionaries, too."

"I know, and I get sick of hearing about it," he said. "For one thing, I think it's nothing but superstition. For another, even if there are evil spirits lurking around, the Bible tells us Jesus has conquered them, and we have no reason to worry."

"I would say there is a reason to worry now," Lester said, nodding at me.

"We get a lot of spells here," Miss Sherry said. "Sorcerer hexes somebody and they want me to cure them. Of course, in virtually all cases it's purely psychosomatic."

"Psycho-what?" Sharon asked.

"Psychosomatic. Power of suggestion. All in the mind." She took the thermometer from my mouth. "Not quite 101. Relatively mild. Eric, I'm going to give you some aspirin and an extra dose of malaria medicine. Sometimes the little parasites slip through. And Roy, I think it might be a good idea to say a prayer in his behalf. It could counteract this sorcery business and make everybody feel a little better."

"You're right. But I think Lester should say the prayer," Roy said.

Lester nodded. To my surprise he knelt on the floor by the bed and placed his hand on my head. Everyone else bowed their heads.

"Father in heaven, we ask you now to heal Eric," Lester prayed. "Cast out any evil spirits, and get rid of malaria parasites or anything else that could be making him sick. We know that the power of Jesus is greater than any other force on earth, Father, and we ask this in his name. Amen."

"Amen," everybody said.

Miss Sherry gave me the pills with fruit juice. "Now, let's let the patient get some rest," she said.

I slept all afternoon, all night, and half the morning. When I woke I could tell the fever was gone, and I felt starved.

Hearing me get up, Ax came in. "Feeling better?"

"Lots." I got dressed and went into the kitchen. "Where is everybody?" I asked, opening the fridge.

"A lot has happened, man," Ax said. "Roy and Lester went back to Wewak."

"Wewak! Why?"

"Some people brought a guy with a busted-up leg to the clinic. A tree fell on it. Miss Sherry said it was a compound fracture. The bone was sticking out and everything."

"Gross!" I smeared butter and jam on a slice of bread.

"Really. Anyway, they had to fly him to the hospital."

"When are they coming back?"

"This afternoon. Then we'll all go back to Wewak," Ax said. "Pam and Sharon are at the clinic with Miss Sherry right now, seeing patients."

I gulped down the bread. "We're not giving up on Muruk, are we?"

"For now. I hate it, too, but it doesn't look like there's much we can do. At least you're not sick anymore."

"Thank goodness."

"You think it was the medicine or the prayer?"

I thought about it, then shrugged. "Maybe both."

"What do you mean?"

"Well, can't they work together?"

He nodded. "I don't see why not."

Just then the shortwave radio crackled in the back room. Ax dashed to answer it. I was finishing my fourth piece of bread when he returned to the kitchen. He was frowning.

"You won't believe it," he said.

"What happened?"

"The plane started acting up. They had to make an emergency landing in some place called Aitape."

"Anybody hurt?"

"No, they're okay."

"What about the guy with the broken leg?"

"There's a hospital there, so he's all right. But Roy said it may take several days to get the plane fixed. Until then, they're not going anywhere. And it looks like we're not either."

12

We hurried to the clinic to tell Pam. A line of patients sat on a wooden bench outside the small building. We peeked in the screen door and saw Sharon, Pam, and Miss Sherry with a patient.

"Pam!" Ax said. "We need to talk to you."

"You boys come on in," Miss Sherry called cheerfully. "Got something I'd like you to see."

A bit nervously, we went inside. The room was large and mostly bare, with a cement floor, a metal examining table, a desk, and a couple of chairs. A native woman sat on the table. Like most women around there, she wore only a skirt. Her right foot was propped on a stool, and her shin was covered in the biggest, most horrible open sore I'd ever seen. It reached from her knee to her foot and oozed pus.

"Tropical ulcer," Miss Sherry said. "One of the most common ailments in New Guinea, next to malaria."

"How did it happen?" Ax asked, his face wrinkled in disgust.

"Starts as a simple cut. Thorn scratch, maybe, or insect bite. Then the heat, humidity, and unsanitary conditions go to work on it, and before long you have a full-blown sore. If it's left untreated for a long period, this is what can happen."

"But why don't they treat it?" I asked.

Miss Sherry shrugged. "No medicine. This woman lives a day's walk from here through the jungle. She waited till the last possible minute to come. I know people at home in New Zealand who are much the same."

She soaked a cotton ball in medicine and handed it to Sharon. "Daub it good," she said.

Sharon went right to work, first smiling at the woman, then gently patting the gaping sore with the cotton. It didn't seem to bother her too much.

"Sharon's getting some good nursing experience," Pam said with a smile.

"She ought to be a natural," Ax said.

"Their father is a vet," Pam explained to Miss Sherry. Then she turned to us. "What was it you boys needed to tell me?"

Ax snapped his fingers. "I almost forgot. Roy

radioed. The plane had engine trouble, and they had to make an emergency landing in Aitape. He said it might be several days before he can get it fixed."

Pam frowned, but she didn't seem as shocked as I'd thought she would be. "That's New Guinea for you," she said.

Miss Sherry smiled. "You can tell Pam's an old hand. Delays are the order of the day over here, aren't they, dearie?"

"I'd better get on the radio," Pam said. "I guess he's staying at Micky Rhodes'. That's a missionary at Aitape. Good friend of ours. You kids can stay here. I'll be back in a bit."

But as she reached the door, she stopped suddenly. "Listen. I hear an airplane."

"You don't think that could be them, do you?" Sharon asked. "Maybe they got it fixed."

Miss Sherry shook her head. "I'm expecting a box of medical supplies. Do you think you boys could run and get it for me? Just bring it back here."

"Sure," I said.

"Come on, I'll go with you," Pam said.

By the time we got to the airstrip the plane had landed and the pilot was getting out. He was young and blond and wore dark blue shorts, white knee socks, a white shirt, and black shoes.

"Hi," Pam said, walking over. "Miss Sherry asked us to get the box of medical supplies."

"Right-oh," he said cheerfully, pulling a large cardboard box from the back. He set it on the ground, then stretched. "One more stop this morning." He peeked in the back at several more boxes. "Got to drop these supplies off at Sisimin for Edward Miller."

"Beg pardon?" Pam said. "For whom, did you say?"

"Edward Miller. You know, the guy they call Muruk."

"But he was just here a couple of weeks ago," Pam said, frowning as she brushed back a strand of her long, dark hair.

"That's right," the pilot said in his thick Australian accent. "Radioed me a while back. Said he planned to hike from here to Sisimin."

"Isn't that a long way?" Pam asked.

The man chuckled. "Is it ever! Must be eighty, ninety kilometers through the bush. I told him he was crazy to try it, but he said there's hunting territory in there that's never been touched."

"When is he supposed to arrive?" Pam asked.

"Didn't say. I'm just supposed to drop the supplies off."

"Did he say where he's going from there?"

"Bloke doesn't talk a lot, you know?" He stretched again and scratched his head. "Well, I've got to be on my way."

Pam seemed deep in thought. "Can you wait just a minute?" she asked. She motioned to Ax and me, and we took a few steps away.

"Boys, this may be our only chance to catch

Muruk," she whispered.

"What do you mean?" I asked.

"I mean maybe we should fly to Sisimin — right now."

"Now?" Ax said. "That's a super idea!"

"Well, it leaves a lot to be desired," Pam said. "I really wish Roy were here, or Lester." She glanced at the plane and bit her lip. "But if we don't go now, we may never get another chance."

"But we don't even know if he's there," I said.

"If he's not now, he should be soon, to get his supplies," Pam said. "And if we can't find him, at least we tried. What do you say?"

Ax and I nodded.

Pam returned to the pilot. "How much room have you got in that plane?"

"Plenty. All I've got left is these boxes for Muruk."

"Have you got room for some passengers? Say, one adult and three kids? We need to go to Sisimin."

His eyebrows went up. "Sure, if you've got the money. We can make room."

Pam looked at Ax and me. "You boys go get Sharon and explain things to Miss Sherry. Take this box of supplies with you. I'll radio Roy. We need to get packed as soon as possible."

"Uh, Pam," I began. "I don't mean to be picky, but what exactly are we going to do at Sisimin?"

She chuckled grimly. "To tell you the truth, Eric, I haven't figured that part out yet."

13

We lifted off from the grassy airstrip and banked over the jungle. Watching the houses fall away, I realized how glad I was to be getting far away from there.

The memory of the sorcerer's eyes made my skin crawl. But whatever he'd tried to do to me hadn't worked — thanks to prayer, medicine, or both.

Also, I was relieved to be away from those diseases. Hot, muggy, dirty, buggy — Yellow River was one unhealthy place. I was looking forward to being in the mountains.

We flew over the muddy Sepik. It reached for miles in both directions, the crookedest river I'd ever seen. Long, curved lakes lay alongside it like baby snakes beside the mama. I couldn't help but shiver.

In the distance stood the mountains in a dark wall. The flat land beneath us began to get crinkly, like an unmade bed. Before long, hills were rising all around us, covered in jungle like something from the dinosaur days. I half expected to see T. Rex chomping a bloody carcass.

We flew into a black cloud and our view disappeared. Rain spattered the windows. The pilot, frowning, studied his instruments, and I wondered how he could tell where we were. The plane lurched and dropped suddenly. Wind! My stomach flew into my throat.

The pilot's knuckles were white on the steering wheel. He glanced anxiously out each window but could see nothing. Everybody else seemed pretty nervous too.

We left the cloud and found ourselves headed straight at a mountain wall! I heard Sharon scream as the pilot pulled the wheel to the left. He guided us into a narrow valley. Sheer walls rose on each side of us. But the pilot seemed calmer now. I realized we must be on course.

Pam smiled and patted Sharon's knee. "They say flying one year in New Guinea is equal to ten years anywhere else," she shouted over the roar of the motor.

"I believe it!" Sharon said.

The valley widened and turned golden in the sunlight as we left the clouds behind.

66

"Wow!" Sharon exclaimed. "That's beautiful!"

"Like Shangri-La!" Pam said, nodding.

A grassy strip lay down the center of the valley. Thatched huts were scattered around it. The massive green walls made me think of the Alps we'd learned about in school.

"Is that Sisimin?" Pam asked the pilot.

"Right-oh!" He circled once before coming in for the landing. As we touched down on the bumpy ground I had the feeling we had flown back in time.

At the end of the strip stood a thatched lean-to. There the pilot stopped. As we climbed stiffly out, people ran to check us out. They were short and dark, and wore ragged clothes probably given to them by missionaries. They stared at us with curious expressions while we unloaded our packs.

The pilot spoke with a headman. *"Dispela bokis bilong Muruk,"* he said. *"Em I stap?"* (This box is Muruk's. Is he here?)

"Nogat," said the thin man, who wore dirty pants and no shirt. He was chewing *buai*. *"Em I stap long Waranini."* (No. He's at Waranini.)

"Waranini i we?" (Where is Waranini?)

The man pointed at the mountains. *"Wanpela de wokabout."* (One day's walk.)

"Longtaim I kamap, bai yu givim dispela bokis," the pilot instructed. (When he arrives, give him this box.)

The headman nodded and spat a stream of red juice into the grass.

"All right," the pilot said to us. "You sure you don't want me to come back and get you?"

"Thanks," said Pam, "but my husband will come. As soon as he gets his plane fixed he's going to fly over."

"All right. Good luck. *Lukim yupela!*" he said to the crowd. (See you.)

They watched as he cranked the motor, taxied down the grass runway, and took off. Soon the plane was a tiny dot in the sky.

"I guess we could hire a guide and hike over to that Waranini place," Pam told us. "Or we could just sit here and wait." A fly buzzed around her face, and she swatted it away.

"Let's hike!" Ax said.

Sharon nodded. "It could be days before Muruk gets here."

A fly landed on my nose, and I snorted. "Hiking suits me," I said.

Meanwhile the people, twenty or thirty of them, were staring at us. Some of them were frowning. Some held machetes.

The thought hit me: What were we doing here? And was it too late to call the plane back?

14

Pam didn't seem nervous, though. She began talking to the headman. They spoke a little too fast for
me to follow, but I could tell she was asking about
hiring someone to help us go to Waranini. While
they haggled, I continued studying the crowd.

Though the people wore clothes, they didn't
seem to understand how they were supposed to be
used exactly. One teen-aged boy wore a pair of old
brown shoes with zippers on the sides. They were
way too big, and he didn't have them zipped up or
even wear socks. Those were the only shoes I saw.
Everybody else was barefoot.

The women all wore skirts, but they didn't all
wear blouses. One just had on a black bra. Some of

them nursed babies. The men wore shorts or long pants, and most of them had on shirts, mostly old and dirty.

I glanced at Ax and Sharon. They were wide-eyed too. None of us had ever seen a place like this — not even Yellow River!

"Okay," Pam said to us. "We've reached an agreement. I'm going to pay four men to carry our packs and show us the way to Waranini."

"Carry our packs? Why?" Ax asked.

Pam nodded to the steep mountainside. "Travel here is hard enough *without* a pack. I'd rather pay a few *kina*, let these people make some money, and make things easier on us."

I was glad, but Ax didn't seem very happy.

"What about Muruk's box?" Sharon asked.

"We'll leave it here," Pam said. "After all, we plan to bring Muruk back here."

"How?" I asked. "I mean, did you ever come up with a plan?"

Pam looked at the ground, then back up at us. "Did I ever tell you kids that Roy and I used to know Muruk?" Pam asked. We shook our heads. "Believe it or not, he came to church a few times. This was several years ago. Roy thinks he just wanted people to think he'd gone straight. That may be, but I think he also had an interest in the Gospel, just a little. I believe I can talk him into giving himself up."

"What?" Ax said in disbelief.

"The guy's dangerous," I said.

Pam shrugged. "Look, folks, I'm dealing with things as they come up. If I change my mind, I'll change my plan, okay?" She glanced at the afternoon sun. "Anyway, it's too late to start today. And the men want to get some of their things together for the hike. We'll leave first thing in the morning — *morning morning true.*"

"Where do we stay tonight?" I asked.

"They offered us a hut, but I'd rather pitch a tent. If we stay in the hut, the mossies will probably get us."

"Mossies?" I asked.

"That's what Australians call mosquitoes. I guess I've picked up some of their expressions. All right, let's get to work."

The crowd watched in amazement as we put up Pam's big blue family-style tent. We put our packs inside and unrolled our sleeping pads and bags.

When we came back out, a man offered us a bunch of bananas. Pam thanked him and told the group we would buy more fruit if they would bring it. Soon we had more bananas, along with pineapples, papayas, and a couple of watermelons.

"Eat your fill," Pam told us. "Might as well enjoy the fruits of the land."

We settled back into the shade of the lean-to and ate. The bananas and papayas were great, but the watermelon wasn't as sweet as the ones back home.

Most of the crowd moved off slowly, but a few people stayed to watch. I saw now that their frowns were just curious, not unfriendly. Whenever I smiled at them, they smiled back enthusiastically, sometimes even laughing.

Some dogs wandered up, scrawny, short-haired, pointy-eared creatures. One had a bloody gash in its shoulder.

"What happened to him?" Sharon asked.

Pam asked a villager, who replied, "*Muruk.*"

"You mean the poacher did this?" Ax said with a frown.

Pam shook her head. "The bird. *Muruk* means cassowary, remember? The dogs probably chased one, and that one got too close."

"Wow," Ax said, studying the nasty cut.

"So what are we going to do all afternoon?" I asked. I didn't want to think about the giant birds.

Pam shrugged. "Just take it easy. We'll need all our strength tomorrow."

"I know," Sharon said. She went into the tent, dug around in her pack, and returned with a deck of cards. "I had a hunch we might need these. Anybody up for crazy eights?"

"Sure!" I said.

"Yeah," Ax agreed.

Pam rose and stretched. "I think I'll nap," she said with a yawn, and went to the tent.

We played cards for an hour or so. When Pam woke, she asked a villager where we could wash up. He told us about a stream nearby, so we

changed into our swimsuits and followed a steep path down from the airstrip. At the bottom, we found a rocky brook with a four-foot waterfall pouring into a small pool. We all waded in and took turns getting under the fall. The icy water felt great.

Later we went to the tent and cooked supper on a campstove while the sun set over the mountains. Everything seemed quiet and peaceful. We could hear laughter and smell woodsmoke coming from the village, which was at the far end of the airstrip.

Since there was nothing to do and nowhere to go, we went to bed early and lay in our sleeping bags talking. It felt like summer camp — except we were in the middle of one of the wildest countries on earth!

15

By the time we finished eating oatmeal and bananas for breakfast, our carriers had arrived. There were four men, plus four women to carry the men's stuff. Big string bags full of sweet potatoes and bananas hung from the women's heads.

We were on the trail down to the stream with the waterfall before the sun topped the mountains. Two men led the way, followed by Pam, holding the shotgun. The carriers moved so fast I nearly had to jog to keep up.

"*Isi isi,*" Pam yelled, telling them to slow down.

We had to cross the stream several times. Sometimes I could step on rocks but other times I had to wade, soaking my boots. Finally the path led up the side of a steep hill choked with vines.

"This is a garden," Pam said, panting. "Sweet potatoes, see? There's so little flat ground they have to plant their gardens wherever they can, even on these hillsides."

The sun appeared overhead, scorching. By the time we entered the shady jungle, I was pouring with sweat. We each carried a small canteen, and I paused to chug.

The trail kept going up, and up, and soon I felt exhausted. Maybe I wasn't well yet. But I noticed Pam and Sharon were breathing hard too. Even Ax looked tired. The carriers, though, were chatting happily, chewing *buai*, sometimes even breaking into song. I didn't see how they could find the breath to sing!

At last we reached the top. There was no view because of the dense forest. For a short time the walking was easy; then we started downhill. That was easier on the lungs but harder on the legs and feet. The trail was narrow and muddy, and several times I nearly fell.

When we neared the bottom, we came to a long log. One of the carriers said something that sounded like "oil." I shrugged and stepped onto the log — and my feet slid like roller skates! Oh, he meant slick as oil! I warned Ax and Sharon, who were behind me, then crossed very carefully.

We stopped at a small stream to rest. The clear

water ran over gravel in deep shade. Pam sat on a mossy log, and I plopped down beside her. Ax and Sharon sat on boulders. The carriers dropped their loads and drank from the stream.

"Well, what do you think so far?" Pam asked us.

"I'm glad we're not carrying our packs," Sharon said.

"Me too," I said.

"What about you, Ax?" Pam asked. "Do you wish you were carrying yours?"

He shrugged. "I could handle it." Then he smiled. "But I'm glad I don't have to."

"How much farther is it?" I asked.

"They said a day, but we can't go their pace, so I'm sure we'll camp on the trail and get there sometime tomorrow."

"Camp in this?" Sharon said, frowning at the deep jungle and steep slopes.

There was no flat ground anywhere. The mountains rose sharply on either side of the stream. And the rain forest was so thick I didn't see how we could pitch a tent.

"We'll find a place," Pam said.

"Is this what it was like when you were on the run from the cannibal?" I asked, remembering Roy's book.

"That was a long time ago. I guess it was like this, only there was no trail, no food, no guides. But we were much younger and had more strength, I suppose."

"I read the book on the flight over," Sharon said. "I liked the part about how you and Roy fell in love."

Ax and I smirked. Pam smiled dreamily. "Yes, God can bring good out of the worst situations. In some ways that was a beautiful experience — and in other ways the most horrible I'd ever known." She shrugged. "Anyway, it all worked out in the end."

"Like the verse," Sharon said. " 'In all things God works for the good of those who love him — ' "

" ' — who have been called according to his purpose,' " Pam finished for her. "Romans 8:28."

"*Yumi go*," said the lead carrier. (Let's go.)

Pam stood. "All right. Let's hit it, kids."

On we went, up and up. In one place a giant tree had fallen, giving us a view of the mountains around us. They looked dark and gloomy, nothing but jungle as far as we could see.

We were almost to the top of the second mountain when the lead carrier dropped his load and hurried back to Pam. He whispered to her, then she turned to us.

"Noa sees some birds up ahead and wants to shoot one," she said. "Do one of you kids want to try it?"

"Why would he want to shoot a bird?" Sharon said with a frown.

"Food," Pam said. "These people get very little meat. They can't go to a grocery store and buy it like you can back home. When they get a chance to hunt, they take it, especially if they've got a gun. Now, which one of you is the best shot?"

"Eric is," Ax said.

Sharon nodded. "He's had lessons."

"A WSI agent taught me for an assignment in Central America," I explained. "I haven't practiced much since then."

Pam handed me the gun and some shells. "I'm sure you can handle it. Just go with Noa and he'll show you where the birds are. We'll stay back here."

Noa waited impatiently. I slipped a shell into the chamber of the single-shot twelve-gauge and followed.

16

Noa stepped off the trail. His bare feet made no
sound. I wished I could say the same for myself,
but as we went down a steep slope I broke some
twigs and once I fell on my rump.

Noa glanced around and motioned for me to
crouch. We began to duck-walk, keeping low. At
last he grabbed my arm and pointed to the treetops.

"Pisin i stap antap," he whispered. (The bird is up
there.)

I saw nothing. Noa looked at the tree and back at
me. He pointed again. I saw movement in the leaves.
Then I spotted a big black bird with a long bill.

"Sutim," Noa said. (Shoot.)

I raised the gun, but the bird stepped behind

some leaves. It seemed to be eating fruit or something. I waited, but my arm got tired and I lowered the gun.

Noa sighed. We duck-walked some more, which hurt my legs. Then he pointed again, and I saw the bird. It was almost straight above us. I sat back, raised the shotgun, and put the bead on the bird's dark body.

It flew to another branch.

I moved the barrel and tried to find it, but it was hidden. I lowered the weapon to rest.

"*Yu laik mi sutim em?*" Noa said. (You want me to shoot him?)

"*Nogat,*" I said.

There it was! I aimed and had a full view. Bracing myself, I pulled the trigger.

The gun boomed. I couldn't see anything for the smoke and falling leaves. Something hit the ground. Noa sprang forward and returned with the dead bird. It was as big as a crow but had a long, curved beak.

"*Kokomo. Arapela i stap antap,*" Noa whispered excitedly. (Kokomo. Another one is up there.)

I handed him the gun. He took it with a happy grin and vanished into the bushes.

I stared at the bird I had killed. Its neck was limp, probably broken. Blood dotted the black feathers, which up close shone with rainbow colors. In a way I was sorry I'd killed it; in another way I was proud. I was a hunter!

The gun boomed again, but nothing struck the ground. Noa returned with a frown and asked for another shell. After a while I heard another shot, then the thud of something falling, and he came back carrying the other bird.

Together we climbed the hill to the trail. Everyone was sitting around talking.

"What'd you get?" Ax said.

"He called it *kokomo*," I said, holding up my bird. "We each got one."

"Hornbill," Pam said. "Lots of meat."

"That's big!" Sharon said. I was glad she wasn't mad that I'd shot the bird.

Everybody gathered around to admire. Two women took the birds and stuck them in their string bags, and we all started hiking.

I soon forgot all about the hunt. The trail kept going up, and by noon when we stopped for lunch I was worn out.

Pam, Sharon, Ax, and I ate crackers with cheese, peanut butter or jelly, plus some raisins and hard candy. The carriers heated sweet potatoes, which I guessed had already been cooked, over a fire.

We took a short rest, then hiked. The trail leveled out some, like we were on top of a ridge, and the walking got easier. The air felt cool up there, probably because we were so high. Deep moss covered everything.

Late in the afternoon we stopped to camp.

"I don't know about you kids, but I'm worn out," Pam said, wiping her sweaty face.

"Me too," I said.

We pitched the tent on a flat area, and Pam started a pot of rice. The carriers built a lean-to and kindled a fire. The women plucked the birds and put the meat into a pot of water over the fire.

Noa came over and asked to borrow the gun. Pam said it would be okay. He took it and hurried off.

Just before dark we heard a shot. Noa shouted, and others rushed out to see what he had. Soon two of the men came back carrying a dead cassowary! It was as tall as a person. One woman followed with a live baby cassowary; another carried a big green egg.

The cassowary was awesome. It had a long black neck with a head that made me think of a cross between a turkey and a dinosaur. Hairy black feathers covered the body, and the legs were long and muscular, with claws like knives.

Whoa!

Everybody was happy now because they had plenty of meat. As Pam, Sharon, Ax, and I ate rice and canned fish, the carriers dug a hole and raked hot coals in, then scraped dirt on top. They plucked the cassowary, cut up the meat and wrapped it in leaves, then placed it in the firepit. One woman put chunks of sweet potato and banana on a large leaf, broke the egg over it, and stirred it around like an omelet. Then she wrapped it up with vine and put it with the meat. They covered the pit with dirt, rocks, and leaves, so everything would bake like it was in an oven.

"They'll cook that all night," Pam said. "In the morning they'll have a feast. It's called a *mumu*."

"Kind of like a Hawaiian *luau*," I said.

"Exactly."

One of the women brought us a big leaf with pieces of the steaming *kokomo*. It tasted like dark chicken meat — yum!

When it was dark, we got in our tent, while the carriers sat around a campfire talking cheerfully. When it started to rain they just scooted under the lean-to and built the fire bigger.

"They sure know what they're doing," Ax whispered.

"Yes," said Pam sleepily, "but I'm glad we have this tent."

Me too, I thought as I drifted off to the sound of voices, and rain tapping on the tent.

17

We reached Waranini the next afternoon. It was just a few huts surrounded by gardens near a river. On the far side were jungle-covered mountains.

The people looked more primitive than the ones at Sisimin. Instead of clothes they wore grass loincloths. Our carriers told them we were looking for Muruk, but the villagers didn't seem pleased.

"Muruk wantok bilong yu?" asked the chief, who wore a pig's tusk in his nose. (Is Muruk a friend of yours?)

Pam appeared thoughtful. Then she said, *"Nogat. Mipela bilong guvman, na mipela kam i kisim em."* (No, we're from the government, and we've come to arrest him.)

I couldn't believe my ears. She was blowing our cover!

But the headman smiled and nodded. *"Gutpela. Dispela Muruk i rascal nogut tru. Em I sutim olgeta pisin long dispela hap."*

"What did he say?" Sharon asked. The man had spoken too fast for us to follow.

"He said Muruk is a rascal and that he's killing all the birds around here," Pam said. "These people are bound to be furious, but too frightened to do anything." She turned back to the chief. *"Muruk I stap we?"* (Where is Muruk?)

The chief pointed to the mountaintop behind us. *"Antap."* (On top.)

We peered back at the jungle-clad slopes. The thought of climbing again made me cringe.

Pam got permission to camp, and we pitched our tent. I unrolled my sleeping bag and lay down.

"You okay, Eric?" Pam asked.

"I don't feel so good," I said.

She touched my forehead. "No fever. I suspect you're still weak from that attack of malaria. It usually takes a few days to recover. I'm surprised you made it this far without any problem, sweetheart."

"But what about Lester's prayer?" I said.

Pam smiled. "It was miraculous. But that doesn't mean you won't ever get sick again. You get malaria parasites every time a mosquito bites you, and they stay in your bloodstream."

"How come you guys aren't sick?"

"Some people have better resistance than others." She shrugged. "Now you just rest. I'm going to talk some more with the chief."

"Yeah, take it easy, big guy," Ax said. "Sharon and I are going to take a look around."

I nodded. All I wanted to do was close my eyes. But when I did I saw rain forest trees spinning slowly around me . . .

Voices woke me.

"Shhh, Ax! He's sleeping," Sharon said.

"But he's got to see this!"

Ax and Sharon were standing outside the tent.

"It's all right. I'm awake," I said.

"Come look, Eric," Ax said. "They've got a pet cassowary."

I sat up, still dizzy. I took a drink from the canteen and went out. I felt stiff and sore all over.

Ax frowned at me. "Boy, you look pale."

"Must be the malaria parasites," Sharon said. "They eat red blood cells."

"This will make you feel better," Ax said.

They led me up a path to a half-finished hut on stilts. A large shape stepped around the corner. Cassowary! I tensed, ready to run.

"It's okay," Sharon said. "She's tame, sort of."

She approached the bird with her hand out, making a clucking noise. The bird eyed her fiercely.

"Careful," Ax warned.

Sharon reached out and scratched the bird's long, hairy neck. It closed its eyes, raised its head, and made a funny purring sound. We laughed.

"She loves to be scratched," Sharon said.

"She doesn't look like the one we saw in the jungle," I said. The bird's feathers were blonde and her skin pale. "Is she an albino?"

Ax shook his head. "Her eyes aren't pink. I guess sometimes they just turn out this way, like a white deer or something."

"Isn't she beautiful?" Sharon said. "I'm going to call her Blondie."

"Better watch out," I said. "You remember those dogs at Sisimin."

"Yeah," Ax said. "And you know what they say. One swipe of those claws can rip your guts out."

"I'm being careful," Sharon said. "But I don't think she'll hurt me. Pam said people raise them from babies sometimes and keep them around like pets. If she were that dangerous she wouldn't be allowed to roam loose."

The smell of woodsmoke reached my nostrils. The sun was dropping behind the mountains, and the shade felt cool.

"This isn't a bad place," I said.

"Lonely, though," Ax said. "I'll be glad when we catch Muruk and get out of here."

"I'd love to stay here a while and study the animals," Sharon said. "Especially Blondie." She gave

the bird a last scratch and rejoined us. Blondie pecked at the ground like a chicken.

Pam walked up. "There you are," she said. "We need to talk strategy."

"What'd you find out?" Ax said.

"I'd hoped these villagers would help us capture Muruk, but they won't. They're terrified of him."

"So what are we going to do?" Sharon asked.

Pam shook her head. "Even our own carriers won't help. They agreed to stay here until we're ready to go back, but when it comes to catching Muruk we're on our own."

"That's fine with me," Ax said. "The fewer there are, the less chance something will go wrong."

"You may be right," Pam said. "Anyway, I suggest we get up at daybreak and go up the mountain. They told me generally where he is. We'll just have to talk him back down."

"Do you really think that will work?" I asked.

"Obviously we're not going to be able to overpower him. Wouldn't be safe. I think if we explain why we're here and tell him he simply can't keep up this poaching business, maybe he'll agree to put himself under arrest."

"But those aren't our orders," Ax protested. "I thought we were supposed to sneak up and ambush him."

"If Roy and Lester were here we might try something like that, or if the villagers had agreed to help.

But one woman and three kids against a man with a gun? No way."

"But we have a gun," Ax said.

"Yes, and it's staying right here in the village while we're gone. I'll never win his trust if I'm carrying a gun."

Ax looked to Sharon and me for support. Sharon just shrugged.

"Eric, I know you agree with me," he said.

I knew what he was thinking: *Grown-ups! This is just the kind of crack-brain scheme they'd come up with!* But I was just too tired to care. I sat down at the edge of the hut. "I don't know," I muttered.

"How are you, Eric?" Pam asked with a frown of concern.

"I feel weak."

"Maybe you should stay behind in the morning. It's going to be a hard climb."

Ax groaned, but I couldn't help the way I felt. "All I know is I need to lie down," I said.

"Sharon, would you mind staying with him tomorrow?" Pam asked. "I hate to leave him by himself."

"Sure," she said. "Like Ax said, the fewer the better."

Pam put her hand on Ax's shoulder. "Looks like it's you and me, pal."

18

In the morning I slept late and didn't hear them leave. Sharon was gone, playing with the cassowary, I figured.

I drank from my canteen and noticed someone, probably Sharon, had left a big papaya right outside the tent. Just right! I peeled it with my pocket knife and ate the juicy fruit. I could feel it boost my energy.

I was about to go look for Sharon when I heard a gun boom way up the mountain. Yikes! Was it Muruk hunting? Or had someone been shot?

Just then Sharon showed up. "Did you hear that?" she asked.

"Yes."

"What do you think it means?"

"Beats me. Our gun is still in the tent," I said.

"Maybe it's just Muruk shooting birds."

"Well, there's nothing we can do about it except wait."

She stared at the mountainside. "I guess you're right. How are you feeling, by the way?"

"Better. Thanks for the papaya."

She grinned. "Sure."

"Where's Blondie?"

"Over by that half-finished hut. I've been playing with her. Training her, in fact."

"Training her? To do what?"

"Come on, I'll show you."

She led me down the path through a tangled garden. When Blondie saw Sharon she came at a run. I almost took off, but Sharon stopped me.

"She just wants her neck scratched. See?"

The bird halted. With her neck outstretched she was taller than we were! Sharon scratched, and I laughed at the way Blondie closed her eyes happily.

"Now watch this," Sharon said.

She pulled a rope from her back pocket and rigged a neat harness around the bird's neck. Then, to my amazement, she swung onto Blondie's broad back.

The cassowary took a couple steps backward, bobbed her head, then stood still. Sharon patted her neck soothingly.

"Awesome!" I said.

Sharon clucked her tongue and tugged the reins to the right. The bird turned and began walking, like a two-legged horse. Sharon rode around the hut and came back.

"Want to try?"

"Sure!"

She climbed down and handed me the reins. Nervous, I swung my leg over and sat on Blondie's back. It was big enough for both of us, but bony.

"Wish I had a saddle," I said. "Her backbone is sharp."

"Scoot forward," Sharon suggested.

I slid up and found that the shoulders made a softer seat. I clucked and dug in my heels — and Blondie took off at a gallop!

"Whoa!" I said, pulling back on the reins. "Whoa, girl!"

She stopped, then ducked her head. I plunged straight down her neck and landed on my butt. Blondie eyed me sternly.

Sharon was trying not to laugh. "You've got to be gentle," she said.

I stood up and dusted off the seat of my pants. "Gentle. Right."

I reached for the reins but Blondie shied away. Sharon took them and handed them to me. She steadied the bird while I climbed back on.

"Easy, Blondie," I murmured. "Easy, sweetheart." I patted her side. "That's a girl. Now come on."

I tugged the reins — gently! — to the right. Blondie turned. Clucking, I urged her forward. We made it around the hut with no problem.

"Nothing to it," I said.

"Mind if I get on too?" Sharon asked.

"Think she's strong enough?"

"We'll find out." Sharon slid up behind me. Blondie took a few steps, then stood still.

"Doesn't seem to bother her," I said.

"Here, it might be easier if I take the reins," Sharon said, reaching around to get them. "You hold onto her neck."

She tugged the reins and Blondie began to walk, awkwardly at first.

"She's getting it," Sharon said.

"This is cool."

We rode down the path to the main houses. When people saw us they ran up laughing and chattering. Little kids squealed happily.

"I'll bet they've never seen anything like this," Sharon said.

"I know *I've* never heard of anyone riding a cassowary," I said. "I don't believe anybody could train one but you, Sharon."

"Oh, Blondie's very gentle."

"Gentle? She's a cassowary! They're natural killers. You're just a whiz with animals."

Sharon urged Blondie into a trot. The bird pranced as if proud to have us on her back — just as we were proud to be riding her.

19

We broke for lunch, then went riding in the jungle. It was peaceful plodding along, Sharon's arms around my waist, Blondie's footsteps quiet in the leaves.

"Don't you just love the rain forest?" Sharon said softly, sniffing the sweet, humid air.

I slapped a mosquito on my neck. "Too many things that bite — and I don't mean just mosquitoes."

"What else?"

"Snakes, crocodiles, stuff like that."

"Oh, Eric. Snakes are afraid of people, and there aren't any crocodiles up here in the mountains."

"What I don't understand is why there are no monkeys and elephants and tigers — not that I'm complaining," I said. "But that animal book we read back home said wild hogs are about the biggest mammal in New Guinea."

"Yeah, the ocean kept them from crossing over," Sharon said. "There sure are some strange creatures, though. Like wallabies."

"Walla-which?"

"Wallabies. I thought you read the book."

"I just skimmed it. I mainly read about the man-eating crocodiles," I said.

"Wallabies are like small kangaroos. Plus there are *tree* kangaroos."

"Too weird." I glanced up into the treetops but didn't see any.

"Look, here's a creek," Sharon said. "Let's stop and soak our feet."

"Feet? I'm going to soak *all* of me." I jumped off Blondie and headed for the water. There was a clear pool just big enough for sitting. I peeled off my shirt, shoes, and socks and waded in wearing just my hiking shorts. Sharon slid off Blondie, removed her shoes and socks, and sat on a rock with her feet in the water.

"Boy, this feels great!" I said, leaning my head back with my eyes closed. "I can't remember the last time I had a bath." I peered at Sharon, who looked pretty grimy. "You ought to come on in."

She grinned, as if I'd read her mind. "Okay." She waded gingerly in, then sat down and ducked her head under, rinsing her hair. It spread out in a blond fan under water.

She came up sputtering. "Feels wonderful!"

I went under too and ran my fingers through my hair. I came up and wiped my face.

"This makes me think of Roy's book, when he and Pam were in the jungle," Sharon said.

"I'm glad it was them and not me."

"What do you mean?"

"Running through the jungle's not my idea of fun."

"I thought it was romantic," Sharon said.

"Romantic! To be chased by a cannibal?"

"Well, they survived. Plus they fell in love. And I think it's so neat that they're still in love. Don't you?"

"Sure." I thought about the book. "I liked the part where the cassowary attacked. Of course, if you'd been along it never would have happened."

"Why not?"

"You would have sweet-talked it like you did Blondie," I said. "Then all three of you would have ridden out of the jungle."

Sharon laughed. "I don't know, Eric. That cassowary was wild, remember? Blondie was already tame."

"She's still a wild animal." I glanced at the big bird grazing nearby.

"Well, I just think you have to treat animals with love and understanding. If you love them they'll love you back." Sharon took a deep breath and looked around. "That's why I'd like to spend more time out here in the rain forest, getting to know *all* the animals."

"Even those worms crawling up your neck?"

"Worms?" She grabbed one and looked at it. Then she jumped up and screamed. "Leeches!"

The tiny, black, wriggling creatures clung to her arms and legs. She batted them away — and bright red blood streamed down her skin.

Suddenly it occurred to me: If *she* had leeches, *I* had leeches.

I jumped up with a yell and saw them on my own body. I raked them off and soon was streaming with blood.

"Are they poisonous?" I gasped.

"No, no. They just suck your blood. We're okay now."

"Okay? We're bleeding to death."

"They've got something in their saliva that keeps your blood from coagulating," Sharon said. "That's why we're bleeding. It should stop now that we've got them off."

"Gross!" I looked down at my chest and stomach. "I'm going to wash off."

"Be careful. They're in the water."

I knelt at the edge of the creek and splashed myself all over. When Sharon saw that I didn't get any more leeches on me, she joined me. Soon we had most of the blood off.

"You still think we should love all creatures?" I asked.

She grinned. "Maybe not *all* of them. But I'm sure even leeches have a role to play in nature somehow."

"Yeah, to make kids like us miserable."

"Hey, Eric, look at this." She cupped her hands full of water and held them up. I looked close, expecting to see some new kind of squiggly thing. Then she dashed the water in my face and danced out of the way, laughing.

"Very funny!" I sputtered. "Just wait till I throw you to the leeches!"

I chased her and grabbed her wet shoulders. She squealed. I started dragging her back to the creek, but she stuck her foot behind my legs and we both tumbled to the ground.

Just then someone came running up. It was Noa, our guide, and he was almost out of breath.

"Mi ben wokabaut antap na mi lukim Muruk i kisim wantok bilong yupela!" (I was walking on top and I saw Muruk capture your friends!) He pointed up the mountain.

Sharon and I stared at each other in shock. Then I noticed Noa was carrying our shotgun and shells. He handed them to me.

"Let's go," Sharon said, getting to her feet. "We'll ride Blondie."

20

Sharon climbed on and I slid in front of her, holding the gun with my left hand and Blondie's neck with my right. Sharon's arms encircled me so she could grip the reins.

"Let's follow the creek up the mountain," she said.

"Right! Just hurry," I said.

Noa watched in awe as we rode away. As we picked up speed, leaves and branches began to whip my face.

"We need to slow down a little," I said. "This undergrowth is thick."

"She likes to run," Sharon said, tugging the reins. "Maybe I can at least get her to jog."

Blondie easily dodged bushes by ducking, but Sharon and I weren't so lucky. It was worse on me since I was in front. Every time Blondie ducked, branches slapped me in the face. And when *I* ducked, Sharon caught it.

But the higher we went, the less brush there was. Before long we were moving okay.

"Boy, I'm glad she doesn't ever seem to get tired," I said.

"Those legs are pure muscle," Sharon said.

"She's fast, too, thank goodness."

"It's almost like riding a horse," Sharon said as Blondie ran with long strides through the forest.

"I think we're getting the hang of it — "

Next thing I knew, I was face-down in the creek. I got up sputtering. Sharon had fallen beside me and looked as surprised as I was.

"What happened?" she said.

"We came to the creek bank and Blondie jumped it," I said. "Only she made it across and we didn't." I nodded to the bank where Blondie stood impatiently.

"I never saw it coming," Sharon said.

I picked up the shotgun and wiped it down with my shirttail. "Me either."

Soaking wet, we clambered up the bank and mounted Blondie.

"We'd better go slower," I said.

"If that's possible," Sharon said. "She's not so

easy to control out here in the jungle. Maybe her wild side is coming out."

She clucked her tongue, and Blondie started off. She went slowly at first, but not for long. She just had to run.

"Oh well," Sharon said. "At least it's pretty open up here."

"It would almost be fun if I weren't so worried about Ax and Pam," I said.

"I know."

"We're almost to the top," I said. "I wonder which way we go."

"My guess is to the left and follow that ridge."

"Let's try it."

We reached the top of the mountain and turned left. The thick mossy ground was so soft I couldn't hear Blondie's footsteps. The air was cool up here, and sweet-smelling.

"Listen! Was that a voice?" Sharon pulled Blondie to a halt.

"A woman," I whispered. "Like Pam."

"And a man. They're arguing."

"I hear Ax, too."

"What do we do now?" Sharon asked.

"First thing I'm going to do is load this gun." I reached into my pocket for a shell. "Oh, no!"

"What is it?"

"These paper shells are wet. Look, it's swollen up and won't even fit in the chamber." I tried every shell with no luck. "I don't believe it."

"Can't you bluff him?"

"Too dangerous," I said. "Let's get closer so we can see what we're up against. Whatever you do, don't let her run."

"Okay."

Sharon urged Blondie ahead cautiously. We moved through the forest until we saw Muruk's camp through the leaves: a green tent, a smoking campfire, and a man dressed in khakis and wearing a wide-brimmed hat. Seated on the ground, tied with ropes, were Pam and Ax.

"He's got them!" I hissed.

"Has he got a gun?" Sharon asked.

"I see two leaning against a tree."

"Two?"

"He probably carries a spare, in case one messes up."

"Think we can ride in fast and grab them?" Sharon asked.

"Yes, but wait till his back is turned." I set our gun down so it wouldn't slow us down. "You handle Blondie and I'll grab the guns."

It was hard to see clearly through the leaves. Muruk was standing in front of Pam and Ax, arguing with them. He was sideways to us.

"I knew Pam wouldn't be able to talk him into surrendering," I said.

"Look! Is he turning his back?" Sharon said.

"Yes. Let's go!"

Sharon dug her heels into Blondie's side. "Go, girl, go!" she whispered.

Blondie darted forward so fast we almost fell off. I couldn't believe how swiftly we were moving, and with hardly a sound!

Muruk just happened to glance back as we were getting close. He wheeled around and stared in shock, like he'd never seen two kids riding a cassowary before. He lunged for the guns, but too late. As Blondie swept by, I leaned out and grabbed both weapons by their barrels.

"Whoa!" Sharon said, yanking the reins.

Blondie stopped so abruptly that I went crashing to the ground, Sharon right behind me.

"Look out!" Ax yelled. "He's got a helper!"

A dark man jumped out from behind a tree and picked up one of the guns. His sudden movements startled Blondie, who spun around to face him. As he raised the gun she attacked. With one powerful foot she knocked the gun from his hands. With the other she reached out with a knife-like claw —

"No, Blondie! Don't do it!" Sharon shouted.

The giant bird's talon struck the man's stomach and ripped downward, slicing him open. He groaned and fell to the ground, hands clasped to his bleeding stomach. Blondie took a step to finish him off, but Sharon snatched the reins and pulled her away.

Remembering Muruk, I grabbed a gun just as he was moving in.

"Hold it!" I said, cocking the hammer.

The wiry hunter raised his hands and backed up.

Keeping the gun pointed with my right hand, I pulled out my pocket knife with my left and tossed it to Sharon. She quickly cut the ropes binding Pam and Ax. Pam quickly hugged Sharon, then hurried to the injured man.

"He's badly hurt," she said. "But the claw didn't cut through the abdominal wall. He's got a chance."

Muruk stared at us in awe — a woman, three kids, and a half-wild cassowary. "Can somebody tell me what the bloody devil is going on?" he said in a thick Australian accent.

"I can, Mister," Ax said. "You've just met Wildlife Special Investigations."

21

We tied Muruk's hands behind his back. Then we bandaged his helper's wounds.

"We'll have to send somebody back with a stretcher," Pam said. "I don't think he should try to walk."

"But what if he gets away?" I said.

"I don't think he's going anywhere, not with this wound."

At Waranini, the villagers met us with shouts of joy.

"*No moa yu sutim pisin bilong mipela*," the chief told Muruk. (No more will you shoot our birds.)

Some villagers went and picked up his helper on a homemade stretcher. They got back around suppertime.

"We'll just have to leave him here," Pam said after checking him out. "He'll be all right, but I don't think he can make the hike to Sisimin."

"Can't they carry him?" Sharon asked.

"They probably can, but I don't know if they will," Pam said. "That's a big job."

"Could he ride Blondie?" I asked.

"That would just make his wound worse, I'm afraid."

"He ought to be punished for his crimes," Ax said.

"I'd say Blondie has already taken care of that," Pam said grimly, and we nodded.

We left early the next morning. The people from Waranini decided to go with us to visit their friends in Sisimin. Muruk walked along with his hands tied behind his back. With such a crowd along there was no danger of his escaping.

Pam, Sharon, Ax, and I took turns riding Blondie. We made such good time that we reached Sisimin by nightfall without having to camp on the trail.

At Sisimin, Muruk was locked in a hut with a guard posted. The villagers did not want him to get away any more than we did.

The next day, all we had to do was wait.

"How long do you think it will be?" I asked Pam after we breakfasted on fresh fruit. We were sitting outside the tent by the grass airstrip.

"There's no telling," she said. "I told Roy to come to

Sisimin as soon as he got the plane working. No one here has seen him, so it must not be repaired yet."

"Then it could be days," Ax said, frowning.

Pam shrugged. "It's possible. In the meantime, why not pretend you're on vacation? Your job is done. Just have fun."

"Yeah!" Sharon said. "Like summer camp. We've got a tent and a swimming hole. There's hiking and riding."

"Riding?" Ax said. "Oh yeah, Blondie."

The giant bird was grazing in the field in front of the tent. In the distance stood the thatched huts of Sisimin. All around towered Alp-like mountains.

Ax shook his head. "I'm tired of hiking, tired of riding, and I don't feel like swimming."

"I know your problem," Sharon said. "You haven't been able to do your karate lately."

He brightened. "You're right. And this field looks like the perfect place!"

We laughed as Ax dashed onto the grass, turning cartwheels. Soon he was punching and kicking, leaping and tumbling.

"He's quite an athlete," Pam said admiringly.

"Oh, he's won all kinds of tournaments," Sharon bragged.

"So what are you two going to do?" Pam asked us.

"What do you say, Eric?" Sharon said. "Ride or swim?"

"We can swim anytime," I said. "But we won't get many more chances to ride a cassowary."

She grinned. "Let's go."

We spent the morning riding. In the afternoon we all went for a swim. We were having so much fun that I was almost disappointed to hear the buzz of an airplane.

"That's Roy!" Pam said excitedly. "I recognize the motor!"

We dashed back to the tent and got everything packed up just as the plane landed. Roy and Lester climbed out.

"Thank God you're all safe," Roy said, hugging Pam and then the rest of us. "I was worried sick."

"No need to worry," Pam said with a laugh. "These kids are professionals."

"Did you catch Muruk?"

"He's locked up right now," Pam said proudly.

Lester smiled. "I knew you could do it."

Roy shook his head in awe. "What happened?"

"It's a long story," Pam said. "I wish you'd been along, dear. You could have written a book about it."

"Yeah," I said. "It was almost as exciting as your first adventure."

Pam smiled. "Almost." Then she gave her husband a long kiss.

We hooted with laughter, but what the heck. It's good to know somebody's living happily ever after.

Don't miss any of these great adventures from the Eric Sterling, Secret Agent, series:

The Secret of Lizard Island, Book 1
ISBN: 0-310-38251-3

Double-Crossed in Gator Country, Book 2
ISBN: 0-310-38261-0

Night of the Jungle Cat, Book 3
ISBN: 0-310-38271-8

Smugglers on Grizzly Mountain, Book 4
ISBN: 0-310-38281-5

Sisters of the Wolf, Book 5
ISBN: 0-310-20729-0

Trouble at Bamboo Bay, Book 6
ISBN: 0-310-20730-4

Little People of the Lost Coast, Book 8
ISBN: 0-310-20733-9

ZondervanPublishingHouse
Grand Rapids, Michigan
http://www.zondervan.com

A Division of HarperCollins*Publishers*